THE BINDING
DAY TRUCE

Allegra Pescatore
J.P. Burnison

Ao Collective Publishing

CONTENTS

"*Out beyond ideas of wrongdoing and rightdoing there is a field. I'll meet you there. When the soul lies down in that grass the world is too full to talk about.*"

RUMI

Night VINE

Elements
PALM

Shifting
GRASS

Plants
FRUIT

Wards
HERB

Illusions
FLOWER

Animals
EVERGREEN

Healing
FERN

Light/en
Mind

The Nine Lands of the Mountain Fell

In the Mountain Fell, each High Fae is born with the powers of their Land and those that border it.

Their Eyes hold their magic, and the deeper the Gaze, the more deadly the Fae. From lightest to darkest: Rose - Copper - Azure - Verdant - Gold - Violet - Crimson - Silver - Obsidian

TWO WEEKS BEFORE WAR'S END

ILYAS

The Mad Queen of Vine jabbed a needle through Ilyas' skin, sewing up the fresh wound in his shoulder. "I wouldn't have needed to punish you, if you had not lost," she said, still flushed from the beating.

Ilyas's large black-and-gray feathered wings twitched at the bite of her words. To avoid earning another lashing, he kept his eyes fixed on the many waterfalls of Cravmor, shining in the sunset's glow. Eye contact was for victors. Ilyas did not deserve it. "I understand, my Queen. You seek only to make me stronger."

The needle dug in again, and Ilyas tried his best not to wince. A medic would have numbed the wound before sewing it, but Queen Maevian Oriset never allowed her beatings soothed away. The care she showed Ilyas was as much a part of the torture as the whip. Her bare thighs straddling his hips, the scent of her arousal, the sultry way she spoke, it was all a calculated torment.

"What have you learned? How will you do better next time?" Maevian asked, tying off the sutures with a vicious jerk.

"I will kill Willow of Herb, my Queen. I will bathe my blades with his blood and toss his body to the Void," he whispered, eager to make this end. The Earthbond that tied him to Maevian compelled his hunger to please her, though Ilyas knew the task was hopeless.

He would never defeat his enemy, and each time he failed, Maevian would tear more of his soul away until Ilyas was nothing but a hollow shell of rage. At least she might be happy then, when she had turned him fully into the monster the rest of the world already thought him to be.

"Very good. If you defeat Willow of Herb permanently this time, perhaps I will even reward you. Our son is nearly grown. He could use a sibling to fight by his side one day," Maevian said, rocking her hips against his.

It made Ilyas want to sob, though he wasn't sure if it was out of pent-up sexual frustration, anger, or exhaustion. After centuries of fighting this bloody, endless war, the last thing he wanted to think about was another generation picking up where Maevian would eventually leave off, especially not one Ilyas was responsible for. "I live to serve you, my Queen." It was the only viable answer. Her pleasure and joy was all that mattered. The alternative... he did not wish to think about.

When Maevian finally left after making Ilyas wash his blood off her body and bring her pleasure with his mouth, the weary warrior stepped onto his balcony and looked out over the sprawling jungles of Vine. Large, feathered serpents twisted lazily in the sunset orange sky, other lesser faeries, small skitterlings, moved through the canopy of trees—shimmering lights like constellations. The roar of the waterfalls soothed some of the lingering ache in his back, and, not for the first time, Ilyas wished that his visits home weren't marred by Maevian. It was so beautiful here.

If only it still felt like home.

WILLOW

Blood splattered across Willow's face as his enemy exploded. There was no time to take joy in the carnage, though. Twisting and flaring his Obsidian essence to give him an added boost of strength, he dodged a sword strike aimed at his head.

Winged Faeries from Vine surrounded him, all in the white, black, and crimson uniforms of the Mad Queen. Willow's own squad was already down, fallen in this reckless push to drive Vine back from Oliban Fortress. Two enemy soldiers rushed him together. Will threw a ward up around himself, Obsidian power sizzling in the air. His attackers bounced off it, stumbling, their eyes—and therefore power—lighter than his. Will grabbed one by the front of his uniform.

Unlike his enemies, Willow held no weapons, nor did he have wings. A pair of glistening, sharpened brass knuckles were all he needed to kill. Terror shone in his mark's eyes as Will trapped him inside the ward. The fear was like ambrosia. It meant that this wretched filth knew death was coming. Did he regret serving the Mad Queen, now that oblivion faced him?

With a grunt, Willow buried his fist in the soldier's chest. The man's eyes bulged, his raised longblade falling from his fingers. Will grinned and created a ward inside his foe's ribcage, expanding it outward with the force of a hurricane.

His prey exploded.

As the pulped remains splattered across the blood-slicked stone floor, Willow turned to grin at the rest of his enemies. "Alright boys, who's next?"

ILYAS

Ilyas found Davaal waiting for him on the road out of Cravmor. His weapons and provisions were packed away into Elsewhere, the pocket of essence attached to a Faerie's soul.

"I'm off to find Asherah. I thought I'd travel with you down to the front lines," Davaal explained as Ilyas joined him. Maevian's Seer was a stocky, perennially smiling man in his early twenties, very much at odds with the rest of the Bloody Six. Maevian's Soulbonded had carried that name since the first battle of the war, but that was several reincarnations ago. As far as Ilyas knew, this version of Davaal had never taken to the field.

Unlike himself and the rest of the Queen's Earthbonded army, the Soulbonded were reborn each time they died. At over two hundred years of age, Ilyas was still young, but at least, when Willow inevitably killed him, Ilyas would get some peace. The Six never would until Maevian's heart stopped beating. "Thank you. The company will be nice."

The march down the Mountain between the Plane of Zenith—where Maevian's Land of Vine lay —and the Plane of Meridian below it was always a rough and exhausting climb. There were paths down the Mountain, but they were cold, narrow, and dangerous.

Early in their journey, a group of Vine soldiers coming back up from the front shared the news that Willow of Herb had taken Oliban Fortress.

"I guess that's where you're going," Davaal said with a sigh. "I don't envy you the fight ahead, my friend. That man won't stop until Maevian is dead. Never tell her I said this, but sometimes I almost hope he succeeds. This war... It's made her into someone I hardly recognize. If you ask me, that's why Ash hasn't shown back up yet. It breaks our hearts to see our Queen become the monster the other Lands accuse her of being."

Ilyas wanted to agree, but kept his thoughts to himself. He did not trust that whatever he said would evade Maevian's ears. Especially when said to one of her Soulbonded. "I can hope Asherah will be rejoining her Queen soon," he said diplomatically.

Davaal looked toward the Lands of Meridian

far below, shrouded under heavy clouds. Considering that Davaal was Maevian's Seer, Ilyas had to wonder if he saw the same war-torn landscape, or if it was the future that furrowed Davaal's brow and hunched his shoulders. "This war is in its final days, Ilyas. Long ago, I foresaw that Willow of Herb would lead to Maevian's doom. It is utterly fitting that in trying to stop him, we've turned him into a monster and damned our own souls in the process. It saddens me that you were forged in that same fire. Yet, so it must be. It is the only way to save Maevian. I will miss you, my friend. We all will."

WILLOW

"What possessed you to throw yourself at Vine like that?" Dwyn, Willow's senior officer, was nearly always soft spoken. This was an exception.

"I knew I could take them." Will squared his shoulders. "And I did. Oliban Fortress is ours again. I grieve the loss of my squad, but their deaths are on you, not me. Maybe next time, send me in without babysitters. I'm the strongest fighter you have, Dwyn. I should be going after Maevian, and you know it."

"Maevian is an Obsidian-Eyed High Queen in her own Land. She would destroy you." Dwyn admonished, "And with your hot-headedness, you would never make it to her without drawing the attention of the entire Plane of Zenith."

Willow crossed his arms, his skin, uniform,

and short brown hair still caked in dried blood. Why bathe when the carnage would begin anew tomorrow? "And what use is having an Obsidian-Eyed warrior like me on your side, if you're going to hold me back while we lose by attrition? Let me do what you trained me to do, Commander. I can take her."

"No," Dwyn replied, walking over to his desk in the cramped tent. "Your new orders are to hold Oliban Fortress. You are to stay and defend that pass until the end of the holidays, so the village below can be fully evacuated. I don't have the damn men to spare defending land we didn't need. You *can* hold your temper for two weeks, right?"

"You're giving our army a *vacation*?" Willow snapped.

"Morale is flagging, boy. Even proud warriors get tired of the carnage, and Binding Day is important to all the Fae—their side as well as ours. There will be no attacks. There never have been during the Binding Day celebrations in all the centuries of this accursed war."

Will wanted to shake the general. "If Zenith is retreating to celebrate Binding Day, we should use it as an opening to destroy them!"

Dwyn gave him a stony glare. "We will not attack soldiers while they are honoring the Mountain. It shames me that you would even consider such a deplorable act. This is why you have no position of authority, Willow. You let your anger get the better of you, and it gets good men killed. If you want to do more, prove you deserve it. Spend the next two weeks thinking about your actions, and how you can justify your behavior when you act with less honor than our enemies. Remember, you are all we have to defend our Lands. If you fall, we fall. Now go cool off, while I see what we can do *without you*."

ONE WEEK BEFORE WAR'S END

ILYAS

Ilyas eyed the storm coming towards the mountain range. Towering over a long valley and weathered by fierce wind, Oliban Fortress stuck out of the landscape like a gray stone giant. Enhancing his sight with his essence, Ilyas saw few warriors defending it. For a large base, the High Fae of Herb had to know that it wouldn't hold against Vine. To another, the sight of an auxiliary garrison would have been uplifting. To Ilyas, it was ominous and could mean only one thing.

Willow was there.

Ilyas's hands itched towards the blades on his belt. The thought that his Obsidian-Eyed foe—a man with the same power as his Queen and Gaze one shade darker than Ilyas'—was there meant that a lot of good warriors were going to die unless he could finally put a blade in Willow's throat.

The storm that had threatened all day finally moved in over the fortress. Lightning arced through the clouds and a freezing wind blew across his back, the first flurries of slow ghosting over his wings.

It seemed that a rare blizzard was about to tear through the valley, which meant his forces would be at a disadvantage. The sky would not be their friend, and with Willow...

This time, either I kill him, or he kills me. I won't return to disappoint Maevian. I will not disappoint my son with another holiday where I'm not allowed to see him. I must end this.

That didn't mean that the handful of men under his command had to risk everything, though. He turned to them. "Hold this path. It is our only retreat out of the valley. This is my fight."

It was the only mercy Ilyas could afford.

Silver essence pooled into his hands, before he raised his arms. Two rays of essence shot forward and slammed into the walls of the fortress. He swept the beams of condensed essence outwards, evaporating the stone in a thunderous explosion, and declaring his challenge in the most obvious way he could.

WILLOW

The wind whipped through Willow's hair, icy and biting as he skidded down the mountainside. He dug his boots into the rough rocks, one hand grasping the gnarled roots of a shrub. It tore from the ground, but slowed Will just enough for him to bend his knees.

Drawing off of the magic of Vine, he enhanced his muscles and pushed off. The leap was fueled by a touch of Obsidian essence. It sent him hurtling up into the frigid air, before plummeting back down toward the valley floor.

Something else was rising just as fast—black and silver wings beating up towards him. Willow grinned, teeth bared and eyes watering as he fell towards his opponent. The Mountain must have finally listened to Willow's prayers. This. This was a fight worthy of his power and skill.

This time, he would kill Ilyas, because Dwyn wasn't there to hold him back. This time, the Mad Queen's Silver Shade would fall, and with Asherah the Red also dead by Willow's hand, the path to Maevian would be clear.

Nothing would stop him now.

ILYAS

The sleet pelted Ilyas' wings as he swooped low. His blades slammed into Willow's Obsidian ward. He struck with a quick one-two, then pushed off. Speed would bring him victory. The warrior had learned long ago that keeping himself in one place when fighting the ward-wielder only ended in pain.

"Still too slow, Willow," Ilyas taunted as he took to the air. His eyes never left his enemy far below. The ice was clinging to his wings now, and if he stopped flying, he knew he would risk losing them to the cold. Speed would save them, too.

"You're the one fighting the clock, little sparrow."

Ilyas dove again, but he purposefully overshot his foe. His knives were sent into Elsewhere before his feet and fists hit the ground behind his target. Touching upon the elemental essence of Palm within his blood, Ilyas opened up the earth beneath Willow. The dirt and rocks groaned and shuddered as he tried to close them in and over the Obsidian-Eyed Fae.

Crack!

The ground broke open as Willow's defensive ward burst outward, expelling him from the prison of stone.

Damn it. He'd have to find a new tactic.

"The only clock I have to beat is yours," Ilyas growled, before taking back off into the air. "Maybe if I can't break your body, I can just break your men."

Shifting direction, Ilyas flew back towards Oliban Fortress.

WILLOW

Snow buffeted against Willow's wards as he tried to catch a glimpse of his enemy in the swirling darkness of the blizzard. He was up on the fortress walls again. The only thing he could see, besides the fog of his own breath within his ward, were the lights in the village below.

He doubted any of his men were still alive. He could no longer hear their cries. The cold seeped into Will's skin, the fire of his own rage insufficient to warm him. Was it midnight yet? Had the truce begun? Or were Vine soldiers descending on the village to punish the people he had rescued just days before?

No time to think. No time to look.

"This way, you spineless moth," Willow muttered to himself as he backed up to the edge of the parapet. "Don't think I don't see what you're doing. The Mad Queen must be desperate if she's sending you in right before the Binding Day truce to avoid retaliation. Don't worry, though. I never forget."

He dodged a blade that came out of nowhere, his opponent using the snow to conceal himself. Coward.

Will jumped back and his right leg wobbled. There was a long gash across his thigh from the bastard's rapid strikes. Healing magic from Fern was already knitting it shut, but that was the least powerful of Willow's five essences.

Enough of this. It's late. I'm cold.

Summoning a burst of Obsidian power, Willow angled himself to have the village at his back, and let go of all the restraints Dwyn had taught him.

ILYAS

They fought surrounded by fallen trees, driven back to the wilderness beyond the fortress walls. The force of the combined Silver and Obsidian essence had torn them up and scattered them. Ilyas grabbed one of the downed trees and threw it at Willow. The blow bounced off his enemy's wards, but sent him sliding backwards. In that pause, Ilyas seized a second tree, and hurled it. Again and again he did this, until Willow was surrounded by shattered timber. With a flicker of magic from Palm, the wood ignited in a furious blaze of Silver fire. He hoped the flames would cook his foe, sheltered within his wards.

The protective barrier around Willow expanded, pushing the burning logs away from him. He rushed at Ilyas, who formed a Silver ward around his own body just in time for his enemy to crash into him. His magic shattered. The backblast of essence tore through his leather armor like parchment. Willow's hands whipped out, grabbing for any part of Ilyas he could reach.

Willow's speed was only a feather slower, but if he managed to grab hold of Ilyas, Willow would tear open his flesh and create a ward within it. Nothing but fine red mist would remain. Ilyas drove a long knife toward Willow's hand, but a ward formed and the blade shattered.

Void curse him!

With a blast of Silver essence, Ilyas pushed air under his wings to launch himself skyward. A ray of Obsidian power caught him through his leg as he tried to gain altitude. What did he need to do to put this monster down? He spun in the air and released five thin rays of Silver essence, one from each fingertip.

Willow's ward vanished as he raised his hand, firing a larger Obsidian ray of essence at him in response. Four of Ilyas' weaker rays met Willow's stronger with an explosive roar that echoed within the storm around them. It was not enough.

Willow's scorching power caught Ilyas in the wing. Ilyas screamed as feathers and flesh shredded. The smell of burnt skin and charred feathers filled the air. Icy wind and snow whipped his blood and screams away as he tumbled towards the ground. A glowing Silver ward formed around him as he crashed into the earth—

Then through it.

Stone cracked. Earth groaned.

Vine and Herb warrior alike tumbled through the collapsed rock of the valley floor, into the depths of a water-hewn underground fissure. Frigid cold liquid engulfed them. The current dragged at Ilyas' legs, his torn wing. His strength.

Not this way. I'll die fighting, but not like this.

WILLOW

Not like this.

Willow gasped as he broke the surface of the raging underground river. Around him was nothing but inky blackness.

What point is there in killing Ilyas, if I won't be alive to kill the Mad Queen?

He lifted his hand out of the water, creating an orb of white light with the illusionary magic of Flower. The light reflected off the choppy waves and bounced around the rock chamber, scattering little spots of refracted brilliance. The orb floated above Will's head as he struggled against the current pulling him downstream.

They were miles from the fort. Willow's powers did not enable him to create fire or warmth. He could escape the river, but the trek to the fortress would end with him frozen. If he died, the Lands that opposed Maevian would be left defenseless.

Dwyn was right to hold me back. I should have retreated. I never should have engaged.

"Where are you, you winged bastard?" Willow muttered. He needed Ilyas' connection to the elemental magics of Palm. It was the only way he might survive.

A motion from up ahead. A wing, then an arm appeared on the surface before sinking under again. Willow pushed off a rock, launching himself towards the Vineman. There were no living reeds or algae to use Fruit's plant magic on, and a ward would only push Ilyas further away. With only one option left to him, Willow drew upon the physical might of Vine to strengthen his body. Stroke, breathe, grab.

He hooked his arm around Ilyas's waist.

A ward exploded outward, launching them up in a spray of water and cracking stone. Willow didn't stop expanding it until they were back into the open air. A second, angled ward sent them spinning over solid ground.

They landed hard, Willow under Ilyas.

When the world stopped spinning and Will could gasp in a breath, he wheezed, "Time out?"

ILYAS

An uneasy truce had been struck: Ilyas agreed not to attack Willow, in gratitude for saving him from drowning; Willow agreed not to attack Ilyas, in exchange for helping him survive the cold. If both of them were to die, neither side would come out ahead. So for the moment, their weapons were set aside.

Several orbs of Silver fire burned around them as Ilyas pulled upon the elemental magic of Palm. It was enough, combined with Willow's wards, to keep the worst of the blizzard off of them, but if they didn't find shelter, they were still going to end up frozen. His good wing was wrapped around Willow's back, as the man from Herb held onto his arm.

"Do you have any idea where the fortress is? Or what's on this side of the structure?" he called over the wind. "I don't know how far we got in the fight."

"Me neither. I hope it's this way. I haven't spent much time on this side of the wall," Willow responded, sounding stubbornly optimistic despite the fact that his teeth were chattering. "You could have stayed in one spot instead of flying around like a gnat."

"You could be easier to kill. If there's anything I've appreciated about fighting you so many times, it's that you've been a stubborn challenge." For Ilyas, that was the closest thing to praise he would give

Willow.

"You're a Void touched lunatic. You know that, right?" Willow's bitter tone almost brought a smile to Ilyas's lips. Almost.

"I'm not the one who's spent his days defending a fortress and not learning the surrounding terrain. Aren't you supposed to be a War Leader?"

"I wish," Willow said, as they had to venture out from the meager protection of a copse of trees, right into the wind. It made every step a struggle, and left them panting until reaching the next bit of cover. "In the opinion of my Commander, I'm too 'volatile' to be put in charge of so much as a puppy. And there was no point in learning the valley. I'm never in one place for long."

The next copse was thicker, providing them with better shelter from the elements. "We should rest here," Ilyas said, looking around. "Can you place your wards around the whole thicket, or are you too weak?"

The Herb warrior looked around, then indicated a boulder between two trees. As he did, Ilyas noticed Willow was holding onto his midriff. There was a darker tint to his coat. "Against there. I'll give us enough room to sit for a while."

Ilyas nodded, and together they moved to the spot Willow had pointed out. Once there, Ilyas cleared the snow from the ground with a powerful gust of air. When he finished, he collapsed against the boulder. Pulling from Elsewhere, two vials appeared in his hands. "Catch." He said, tossing one to

Willow. "Rejuvenation potion from Fern. Once we've recovered some, we'll make it the last bit of the way."

He didn't tell Willow what he had done for those two small vials, the battles he'd had to win to earn the right to faster healing—to a chance at life.

Willow uncorked his vial with his teeth. Swallowing his potion in one go was swiftly followed by a series of coughs and splutters. "How old are these? They're rancid!"

Choosing not to answer, Ilyas popped open his own vial and drank it. It tasted like the smell of rotten eggs and milk, with just a hint of apple. He leaned forward, head between his knees. "How badly did I get you?"

"One of those thin rays, just before the ground gave out," Willow grunted. Then he looked over, and quietly asked, "How's your wing? That looked rough."

"You've given me worse injuries. I'll recover with time." Ilyas told him, taking shallow breaths to keep from being sick. He was silent for a while as he let the sensation of flesh and muscle knitting back together overcome him, then, "Your commander is right. If you could keep your temper under control, I'd never be able to beat you. I've learned to target everyone around you and knock you off your feet." He should not have said those words, but with Binding Day looming, it hardly mattered anymore.

"Yeah...I've learned that the harder it is for my commander to beat something into my head, the truer it tends to be."

WILLOW

"She looked sad, this time," Willow said, as they trekked along the frozen creek bed, the looming fortress finally visible in the distance through the mellowing storm. "Asherah, I mean. I've killed her several times now, and every time before she had this gleam in her eyes that promised her return. This time, she looked tired. I think I'm tired too."

Willow's side was still bleeding, but the tonic from Fern was working, repairing the interior damage that he hadn't felt until thawing out after their dunk in the river.

Looking over, he frowned, concerned, as the Vineman winced again. "Truth be told," Ilyas said through gritted teeth, "We're all tired, Willow. I've been fighting this war for most of my life, and none of us knows when it will end. I don't even think Maevian does anymore."

Willow glanced down at their feet, each step a slog through the snow. Their essence and physical strength was all but drained in the battle to keep warm and survive the storm. "Do you ever think about what you'll do after the war, and realize that there is nothing there? That you can no longer imagine it?"

The older soldier laughed a bitter laugh. "I've considered what it could be, but I know how this war ends for me, Willow of Herb."

"And what's that? The war is all I've ever

known, ever since Asherah came to kill my family. I think part of me fights so hard and rushes in because I'd rather die ending this, than survive to see what's on the other side."

"There are two points there. Your family was not the target, you were."

"And yet they're the ones who died," Willow snapped.

Ilyas turned and raised his eyebrows at Willow. "Asherah refused to kill you. She refused to kill a child. The other point is that you still have a future, no matter how this war plays out. Regretfully, Maevian's victory is only a feather better than her defeat at this point for me."

"What do you mean? Aren't you crazy about her? I've heard you're her lover, not just her weapon." Willow wasn't quite able to keep the disgust out of his voice.

"I am her weapon of justice and vengeance," Ilyas said flatly. "Every warrior in her armies has been Earthbonded to her, whether they wanted to be or not. She chose me as her... stud, not her lover."

Willow's scowl abruptly vanished. He looked over at Ilyas. "They say she's vicious to those closest to her..."

"If I don't kill you or take the fortress, I will spend the holiday being tortured and denied the right to see my son. Vicious does not speak to half of what the Obsidian High Queen has become." His tone was still flat. "This war will be the death of me, Willow of Herb. I have accepted and embraced that fate."

"Then why do you fight so hard?" Willow asked.

"For the same reason you do. It's all I know."

ILYAS

They had grown quiet. The bitter truths of the war weighed heavy on both men. "If I wasn't here to try to take the fortress by surprise before Binding Day, what would you be doing these next two weeks?" Ilyas asked.

They were nearing the base of the monolithic fortress. The smells of smoke still hung in the air from Ilyas' attacks earlier. The blizzard had mellowed into a steady, gentle snowfall, downy flakes catching in their hair and eyelashes.

"I was told to spend the holiday thinking about my choices and how my impulsivity keeps getting good men killed. Honestly, I was thinking of just watching the village beat the drums and drink myself silly. Maybe pour a cup out for those who aren't with us anymore," Willow said, voice heavy with melancholy. "What about you?"

"The only thing that makes me smile anymore. Ashan turns twelve this year and will soon start training in earnest if I don't miss my guess. Assuming Maevian allows it, I'll be teaching him." A small smile formed on his lips thinking of the young man with a Golden Gaze already, and darkening every few years. Ashan was going to be strong when he became an adult.

"Is he named after Asherah?" the Herb Faerie asked. "Aren't you scared he'll just turn into another warrior like us and her?"

Ilyas looked at him, not understanding the last question. "All of the cultures of Zenith are warriors. It is our purpose to protect the Mountain Fell from the Voidtouched. If he wasn't to be a warrior like us or Asherah, he would not be able to fulfill his duty to his people." He rolled his eyes. "Don't tell me you believe your side's story that we are all Voidtouched monsters intent on conquest?"

The walls of the fortress were only a hundred yards away. They slowed, then stopped before Willow answered. "What else is there to think, when for generations the duty to your people has included invading mine?"

Ilyas sighed and shook his head. "You wouldn't believe me if I told you. No one has in the past." It was disheartening to know how true that was. He had been there and witnessed the attempts to prove who was truly the guilty party of this war. He had seen a great and noble cause take shape, and later watched it burn in the fires of vengeance until there was only ash.

WILLOW

"This is the end of the line, isn't it? We've made it back," Willow said, as they climbed the last step onto the empty fort's walls. "What happens now? We start fighting again?"

Considering that Willow still had an arm around Ilyas's waist, and they were both leaning heavily on each other to stay upright, it seemed like such a futile question. Yet they both knew it had to be asked. "If you don't kill me, you won't get to see your son or teach him to fight, right? And if I don't kill you, you'll continue protecting Maevian, and this war will never end."

Ilyas looked between them. "If you are able to throw a punch, I'll consider it."

"Good thing no one's here to see. This is likely to be pretty pathetic." Willow carefully helped Ilyas sit on one of the raised walls, then stepped away. In the light of the fires that still smoldered from their earlier fight atop the fortress, Willow saw just how ragged the Vine warrior looked. Wing soaked in blood, hair a mess of melting snow, shoulders hunched.

Willow doubted he looked any better.

"So how do we do this?" Willow asked. "On three, or something?"

I could probably take him. His wings don't work. All I'd have to do is knock him off the wall.

Willow examined the traces of essence he had left in his reservoir. His Obsidian Gaze gave him the edge, but would he have enough power to keep himself alive until help came?

More importantly, did he have the mental fortitude?

It doesn't matter. I still have to kill him.

"Yeah. On three."

Down in the village, far below, fires were twinkling. People would be gathered together, ready to beat the drums that welcomed Binding Day and nine days of peace. It had to be close to midnight. In fact, Willow was surprised they hadn't already started.

"One." He counted, widening his stance. Ilyas squared his shoulders.

"Two," the Vineman said.

The light snowfall would have been quiet and peaceful. Only their heavy breathing broke the tranquility.

"Three."

Neither man moved. Down in the village, the drums began.

Binding Day had arrived.

ILYAS

Ilyas took the chipped mug Willow handed him as he looked down over the village at the base of the valley. They were situated in a small room near the top of the fortress. The reason the two had chosen such a chamber was because it was the only one with the view they wanted that still had all four walls. "To the peace of Binding Day," he said, offering a sober salute to the holiday before taking a long sip of brandy. It had earthy tones from Herb, and warmed him from the inside out. The fire in the hearth took much of the chill out of the air. It had taken the last of his essence to light it and give them the heat they'd need to survive the night.

Willow, who had returned with a pile of moth-eaten blankets, took his own mug and raised it as well. "And not being frozen solid."

Ilyas's chuckle was devoid of any mirth. "I have some blankets stored in Elsewhere that are... substantially warmer than those. Once my reservoir refills with essence, I'll pull them out."

"Eh, I hardly notice the holes anymore. Besides, I thought all you stored in your Elsewhere were weapons to chuck at me when I least expect it." Willow sat down next to Ilyas, on the opposite side of the fireplace. From below, the faint sounds of holiday music still drifted on the wind. "Like that damn spiked chain you got me with a decade or so back."

Taking a sip of his brandy, Ilyas shook his head. "Consider how large a weapon actually is, and then how large a couple blankets are." He sighed softly, remembering the fight. "You know, that battle was the victory when Maevian decided she would allow herself to get pregnant. The news of you being carted off the battlefield mostly dead made her the happiest I had seen her in decades."

Willow gave him a tired smirk. "Oh yes, so glad to know my sworn nemesis gets off on me almost dying." Then, more quietly. "What's it like, having a Ruler you're bound to?"

The Vine Warrior stared into his mug. It wasn't a Soulbond that had claimed him, but the threat of more pain that had led him to agree to an

Earthbond in the center of Vine's Ring. There wasn't much he could remember about his life before that day, just the terror and pain that had come again and again until he had submitted to Maevian and made her the core of his existence. "It... I am not the person to ask that of..." he said softly. Had Ilyas any more tears, he would have shed one.

Willow took another long sip, looking out the window. "Asherah, I assume? The woman who dies over and over, only to come back to her Queen? Does the Mad Queen torture her too? Or just her Earthbonded?"

Ilyas did not respond for some time. In the quiet, the sound of cracking wood within the fireplace and the drums down in the village seemed louder. Peaceful, in a way neither of them had ever known. "How I understand it, for Maevian to torture her Soulbonded would be to torture herself. Considering what Asherah and Maevian have been through already... There is no need for her to torture any of them." Ilyas stared deep into his mug before drinking the whole thing straight. He spoke again shortly after, "You won't need to worry about Asherah anymore. I have the feeling she's not coming back. Not this time."

Willow's whole posture sharpened. Then, like the lingering high note of a song, it broke. His shoulders hunched, and he leaned forward, resting his elbows on his knees. "Lucky her."

They sat without speaking, the high-spirited drumming down in the village shifting to a melancholic choral tune. They were too far away to hear the words, but Ilyas recognized it. It was the song for the darkness beneath the Mountain, where the earliest Fae had cowered, waiting for the light of dawn for nine interminable days. At sunrise in nine days' time, offerings would be made and families would gather to give thanks for the Lands of the Mountain, and the Rulers who gave them life.

"What will she do to you, when you return without my head?" Willow asked.

"Honestly... I cannot say. Her moods are quicksilver these days." A deep sigh followed those words. "There is a different option. You could always join her. You are the only thing standing between her taking Herb. You could end the war and give her the Lands she needs to scale the Mountain."

Willow looked away. "You know I can't do that."

Ilyas sighed and reached for the bottle. "Yeah. I do."

WILLOW

They stood once more on the walls. The sun was shining, the sky clear. The wind blowing through the valley was still icy. Below, in the village, the celebrations were over and the evacuation had begun. Soldiers from Herb were making their way up the path toward the smoldering fortress.

"You should get going," Willow said, turning to look at Ilyas. "It would be best if my people didn't find you here."

The Vineman nodded, but didn't move. "What will you tell them?"

"The truth," Willow said, slipping his hands into his pockets for warmth. "That I thought about what it cost to take it, and agree that it's not worth the manpower to defend. Then I'm going to go take the holidays... off. I have a lot of thinking to do. I don't think I'll be showing my face until the truce is over." Will paused briefly before continuing. "Tell your Queen the fortress is hers, and you sent me running. Spend the holiday with your son, Ilyas. All I ask in return is that you make sure that these people have a village to come back to after the war. They don't deserve to lose everything because we decided to get into it on their doorsteps."

"I will do what I can, you have my word," Ilyas said heavily. "I will see you after the truce, then. I promise I won't throw a chain at your throat next time."

"I make no such promises." Willow's lips turned up in a smile, and he extended his hand. "Until we meet again."

Ilyas' hand met his in a firm shake. "You may try, but we both know you still won't be quick enough. Maybe you'll have better luck when you're not quite so young and impulsive."

"Don't count on that, old man."

WAR'S END

ILYAS

Ilyas turned from watching his son sleep. The gangly pre-teen had spent the day getting the hang of using a long hafted blade without tripping over the butt end. His first Soulbonded, Satricia, another warrior woman from Vine, slept on a cot next to her King's bed. They had become Bonded only a few hours after Ilyas had left to go fight in Herb, and the two had been inseparable. Now that they had found one another, it was proof that Ashan was a Fae King, who would come to rule a portion, if not a whole Land, himself.

Ilyas had spent the days since returning training both Ashan and Satricia in weapons and tactics. Their eyes were both Golden currently, and Ilyas could feel the reservoirs of essence in each of them growing as they learned to understand their own strength.

Ilyas, come to me. Maevian's voice caressed and stroked his mind. A shiver went up his spine. Pulling upon his essence, strength flooded through his body. A trail of silver misted out behind him as he raced through the palace. It wasn't that he wanted to rush, he wanted to drag his feet, but he'd had lessons in what would happen if he tarried.

He entered her chambers to find Maevian naked, wearing only a few decorative slim chains. Her wings fluttered behind her lazily. This time, she was situated near a table bearing a charcuterie board of meats and cheeses, and goblets of fragrant wine. Her chambers smelled of orange blossoms and hibiscus. All of it was designed to put him at ease and let him know he had done a good job.

"I promised you a reward," she purred. Maevian sounded almost … happy. Simmering beneath the pleased emotions, though, was rage and pain, anticipation and … he sensed loneliness from her through the Earthbond. In the days since he had returned, none of her Ring had been seen within the palace. Yet, underneath all of that. He could smell *Her*: the scent of the untamed jungle and blood.

Trepidation warred with desire as he approached his Queen. Pleasure and comfort were his rewards for a victory that he had not been certain she would accept. Her wings wrapped around him as her hands pulled him into her embrace. Their lips met in a hungry frenzy of passion. After a moment, the Obsidian-Eyed Queen dragged him back to her bed.

Maevian's hands tore the clothes from his body, nails digging into his flesh. His fingers slid along her skin, scarred from her own battles as befitting the Warlady of Vine.

Throughout the passionate rutting, though, his mind was elsewhere. Talking with Willow and

Davaal. Asherah no longer returning. The noble call of a war for justice he had felt when younger. The ceaseless battles for the Mountain wearing him down.

Ilyas looked down at her, Obsidian eyes closed in bliss, and he finally saw the truth. Asherah not returning was just the start, and it was clear now. There was no justice in this war any more. Just vengeance, madness, and death.

I'm sorry, Ashan, he thought, closing his eyes and gathering his courage.

Calling upon the full force of his connection to the magic of Vine, his essence poured into his body. He could not will a blade into his hands, but with an alacrity born of centuries of war, his fingers closed around Maevian's throat. Her lips parted. Before a word could escape them, he began to squeeze.

The Earthbond erupted in pain as fury filled Maevian's Obsidian Gaze. The Queen's wordless scream of rage thundered across his mind. Her nails dug and ripped through the skin on his arms and hands, trying to pull them from her throat. Obsidian essence condensed around him, stabbing into his shoulders and back while all of his power went into squeezing the life out of the woman who had tortured him for decades.

The Earthbond rippled and bucked. Through the roar of Maevian's essence, Ilyas could hear shouts outside of the windows. Alarms were raised as all of the men and women that Maevian had forcibly Bonded to her felt her fury and pain. The Land itself reacted to his betrayal, trembling and shaking.

His teeth dug into his own tongue, wings fluttering, twitching, as though Ilyas were the one dying. His fingers didn't relent as he strangled the life from Maevian Oriset, the Mad Queen of Vine. The oath he had sworn centuries ago to serve and protect her shattered. The shards stabbed and tore through his very soul, rending it into tattered shreds.

The bells and shouts stopped. Maevian lay motionless. Ilyas could not breathe.

Then cries. Wails in the distance. Thousands of Earthbonded united in the unexpected grief of losing their Queen.

Ilyas rose, shaking, his hands and wrists oozing blood. His back was a mess of burns. Charred flesh and feathers replaced the sweeter smells of orange blossoms and hibiscus. His ears were ringing, a single buzzing tone drowning out all else. He looked down at Maevian's corpse and realized that if he were found, he'd wish he were dead along with her.

He had to run.

With tears in his eyes, he fled out the window and took to the night sky. A trail of Silver essence was the only thing left in his wake.

WILLOW

Willow was overseeing the last of the villagers making their way across the treacherous mountain pass into the protection of Herb's primary wards when he got the news.

"The Mad Queen is dead! The war is over!" The cry carried up from below, along with the sounds of music. Of celebration.

Willow leapt onto a boulder, looking about for the source of that cry. There. A messenger in the uniform of the Meridian-Nadir alliance, her hair blowing in the mountain wind. It took a few minutes to get to her through the villagers, who had stopped in shock. When he did, the messenger looked up at him, beaming.

"What happened?" Willow snapped. It was the last day of the truce. Had Dwyn launched a surprise assault? If so, would the war really be over? Wouldn't the Bloody Six avenge their Queen?

"Maevian Oriset is dead. She was killed by one of her own. The news is spreading like fire. The Mad Queen's Silver Shade strangled her in her bed. The Bloody Six are nowhere to be found. Vine is leaderless, all her Earthbonds shattered. They are retreating and— Wait!"

Willow didn't. He shoved the messenger aside and launched himself off the side of the Mountain, counting on his wards to slow his descent. He had to get to a Faerie Ring. He had to get to Vine.

Less than four hours later, Willow appeared in a ring of standing stones covered in vines and surrounded by rushing rapids. He struggled through the water, following the map Dwyn had just given him, and emerged from a cavern into the muggy heat of Cravmor, Vine's capital. Waterfalls surrounded a lush valley with high cliffs, vegetation tumbling down the sheer slopes and around the stately buildings.

It was eerily quiet for a city. Deserted. Those who remained sat in corners weeping. Willow wandered the terraces and halls of the stone palace, his essence searching for the deep power of Ilyas's Silver Gaze. Instead, he was drawn to a room where a youth knelt beside an altar, upon which rested the body of Maevian Oriset covered in a shroud.

Willow stopped in the doorway. The youth's shoulder shook with tears, but when he straightened and turned to face Willow, there was no tremble to his voice or fear in his Crimson eyes. "Have you come to kill me?"

"Are you Ashan?"

The boy nodded. In his hands, he held the crown of Vine, the points digging into his flesh. In the scent of his blood, Willow could smell his essence—that of a King. The last he had heard of this boy, he'd only had a Golden Gaze. They did deepen with age or trauma, but to make so large a jump hinted at truly fearsome power to come.

He could pick up where his mother had stopped.

Willow should kill him.

Then again, Asherah should have killed Willow.

"If you're here to end her line, do it already." The youth challenged. In his face, Will saw Ilyas's same stoic determination and courage. "We both know I can't stop you."

Willow shook his head and turned away. "No, kid. I'm not here to kill you. I think my days of killing are over."

ILYAS

'Oathbreaker! Murderer!'

Maevian's voice continued to whisper vileness into his head as Ilyas tried washing his hands for the fifth time in a river. They were clean, and had been clean when he'd started, but he couldn't stop feeling like they were coated in blood.

His allies' blood, those Maevian had forced him to kill for her amusement.

Her blood.

It wasn't just the loss of Maevian that caused tears to stream down his face. It was the way the hole in his very soul where the Earthbond had been tore at Ilyas, breaking itself open further and further with each heaving sob. That void threatened to swallow him. Why did he want to survive? He should have let the warriors of Vine slaughter him when they had the chance.

Now, he was so... so desperately alone, and hollow.

Pulling his hands from the stream, he stared at them. They were clean, without a speck of dirt or blood. Yet he felt it. *'That's how you killed me. With those two hands. Oathbreaker. Murderer.'*

His wings curled around him as he dug his fingers into his scalp. The words were searing brands upon his soul. Never had someone been able to break an Earthbond, and since breaking his, Ilyas knew why. The oath he had sworn—to protect and serve Maevian—burned through his flesh and stabbed into his mind. It had been days since he had done the impossible, and he felt like it had been years.

"Ilyas?" A voice broke through his spiraling panic. A voice he recognized. One that had tried to kill him time and again. Ilyas didn't put up a ward. He welcomed Willow's voice. The peace it promised. Release.

Arms wrapped under his and hauled him to his feet.

"Up you get. We have to go. You left a trail an idiot could follow. Time to disappear."

Ilyas didn't even know where he was, but he was too weak to fight. There wasn't anything left to fight for. "G-go?" he asked between gasping breaths. Where would he go, and why? It didn't matter. He was limp in Willow's arms, neither fighting nor helping.

It was fortunate that they didn't have a long way to walk. Willow guided Ilyas into a dense patch of trees, where Ilyas saw a wild faerie ring of mushrooms. As soon as the two men stepped into it, the world around them grew misty. A few minutes later, it cleared and they were no longer standing in Vine.

"Hmm... looks like we're in Grass. Might be far enough," Willow muttered, dragging Ilyas out of the ring. Helping him to the ground with his back against a warm rock, Willow crouched in front of him. From Elsewhere, he called in a bulging bag, and placed it next to Ilyas. "Food, some clothes, enough money to get you started."

When Ilyas didn't respond, Willow snapped his fingers in front of Ilyas's face.

"Stay with me. You just ended the war. Your side might be hunting you, but ours is celebrating you as a hero. You're still alive. Your son is alive. You've spent your whole life fighting to live. Now's not the time to stop."

None of that was right. He was no hero. He could feel Maevian's cackling laugh, recalled from when she would flay the flesh from his body. He shivered, imagining the feel of her knife. Yet as painful as it was, he wanted to feel it again if it meant she were back. "Leave me…" he moaned, openly weeping for his lost Queen.

"Can't do that. I'm the only one allowed to kill you. If you waste away out of grief and guilt, I will be *seriously pissed.*" Willow pulled out a flask of water and pressed it to Ilyas's chapped lips. "Now drink some damned water, eat some food, and *stay alive.* I refuse to be the only one of us that has to figure out how to live beyond this war."

10 YEARS AFTER WAR'S END

WILLOW

It was a decade after the end of the war when Willow ran into Ilyas again. Will's hair was longer than in his military days, bloodstained uniform traded out for a shabby coat and sturdy hiking boots. Some days, Willow still reflexively called his weapons in from Elsewhere at sharp noises, but he was getting better. It had been over three years since he had last lost his temper, and even that had only resulted in a broken bone. Dwyn's lessons in self-control were finally paying off.

It was just after Binding Day, the snow still crisp and the air fresh this close to the Mountain. Oliban Fortress had not been rebuilt, but the rubble had been cleared and used to rebuild the town below. Willow had come, like he did every year, to sit on the walls and look down upon the valley.

This year, he found Ilyas doing likewise.

Sitting down next to him, Willow did not speak. When Ilyas passed him the bottle of brandy, he took it and swallowed a burning gulp, then handed it back.

Ilyas continued to stare down at the village. He hadn't been much of a speaker before, but the man who had hunted him for so long was so quiet and unmoving that Willow thought he hadn't breathed. His hair was longer and unkempt, and he didn't wear a uniform, armor or weapons. The Vineman even looked thinner, like he hadn't been eating as well as he should.

"So?" Willow said at last. "Anything new?"

"You're still loud enough to be heard a mile away," Ilyas said before another swig, a different tone in his voice than Willow had remembered, "I'm surprised that you haven't corrected that in ten years."

"Subtlety was never my strong suit. You look like shit." Willow took the bottle back, gulped down another burning mouthful, then called in the bread and cheese he had stored in Elsewhere. Setting the food between them, he eyed the other man. "Guessing the holiday isn't the party for you that it is for the rest of the world?"

Silver eyes looked up at him and Willow twitched. Ilyas had always been stoic and cold, but now his eyes were completely devoid of life.

"Still not as much of a thinker, either." Ilyas sounded so... hollow. That was the tone he had picked up on earlier.

Will's smile fading, he looked down at his lap. "I had hoped you'd find something new to live for, after all these years."

"Have you?"

Willow shifted uncomfortably. "For a time. I've been looking for the Bloody Six. They're still out there. I intend to find them, bring them to a Ruler for judgement, and then... well, I guess the ethical thing would be to turn myself in as well. I caused a lot of needless bloodshed. I should be held accountable."

"Leave the Bloody Six alone. Trust me, they may be the only ones as miserable as I am." Ilyas shook his head slowly. "The wrong people have been killed and suffered enough. If I knew I could, I would put an end to those who deserve it. The Bloody Six and you are not the culprits."

"But we are still culpable. The way I see it, the only one here who earned his freedom is... you."

Ilyas grunted before taking another swig. "I don't see it," he muttered. The Vine warrior had just lifted the bottle to his lips again when it slipped through his fingers to plunge to the ground far below. Before Willow could ask what had happened, it hit him too.

A sudden feeling, not unlike a thousand small whispers, slipped into him, tugging at his head and heart to climb the Mountain. To go to Zenith. A call he had never thought he would feel, a Ruler tugging at his soul, drawing Willow close. The sensation was pleasant, filling him with hope and warmth.

He glanced down and saw Ilyas staring up, just like he had been. Unlike his own feeling of wonder and joy, the older man's eyes were filled with dread. He was trembling, his wings wrapped around him as if to protect him from the call of their Ruler. "No... Void above... No... " he whispered, hugging himself.

"You felt that too?" Willow's heart was pounding faster than it ever had in battle. He squeezed his eyes shut. At once his mind was filled with a scene he had never beheld. A dense, dripping jungle. Small hands trying to make a fire. A scream.

"I... I did." Ilyas shivered. "You can have them. I do not want another Ruler."

"Damn it. I think they need help." Willow was already on his feet, the urge to go find the source of that tug almost more than he could resist. He looked down at Ilyas. "We need to go."

"Then go. I'll find another cave to hide in. Even if I had the desire to, I am no good to any Ruler. Not after her." He curled up tighter around himself.

Ilyas strangled his Queen. The thought floated up unbidden. *He could hurt this one too.* Another vision. A young face reflected in Verdant eyes. Flushed cheeks, blue hair sticking to them with tears. Blood. Danger.

Willow's fingers twitched. The image of binding Ilyas's wings in a ward and tossing him into the valley pulled at instincts he had tried to bury for ten years. Clenching his fists, he pushed the desire down. "Come with me, Ilyas. Help me find her. Protect her."

Ilyas looked up at him. "Willow, you aren't thinking." He almost sounded like the Ilyas of old, the calculating general that had bested Willow in tactics and was one of the only people to beat him in a fight. "You can waste your time trying to convince me to go where I won't, or you can go save her. I don't want another Queen, especially one who calls to what remains of my soul. I won't let myself get trapped again, or put my fate in another's hands after finally breaking free. I refuse."

Feeling the pull toward a Ruler at last, Willow thought he understood: why Ilyas had fought for all those decades, why the Bloody Six had reincarnated again and again to return to a Mad Queen. If his Ruler turned out to be another Maevian, would Will be strong enough to do what Ilyas had?

No.

But someone needs to be.

"Then run, Ilyas. Keep your distance… and if I ever become like you were… or like the Bloody Six were…"

Their gazes connected. "Then we'll meet on the battlefield once more. Goodbye, Willow. If the Mountain and Void are kind, may we never meet again. I hope you find everything you're looking for, and that this Queen is who you deserve, and not another Maevian Oriset."

Willow turned away. "Goodbye, Ilyas." He was at the stairs when he looked back over his shoulder to say, "For what it's worth… I think I would have liked to be your Bond Brother."

AND NOW A SNEAK PEEK AT

A Bond of Thread

BOOK ONE OF THE MOUNTAIN FELL

"What do you wish for?" the Peddler said,

"A necklace of gold? A needle and thread?

Be it big or be it tiny, I have what you seek.

I'll cut you a deal for something unique."

"I'm searching for freedom," the little Queen cried,

"An end to my grief and a way I can hide.

Keep all the needles, the thread, and the gold,

All that I want is the chance to grow old."

"You're lucky you met me," the Peddler declared,

"I've got what you asked for, so do not be scared.

I'll give you your freedom, but it comes at a cost.

So what will you give, to escape what you lost?"

I

TO CATCH A MOUSE
Ilyas

Ilyas the Oathbreaker needed a mousetrap.

His name alone still brought terror to the hearts of all who heard it. He had commanded the armies of the dread Queen Maevian Oriset in her war of oppression, had slaughtered thousands of her enemies, and even killed her in the end. It was, therefore, irksome beyond reason that this mouse had evaded him for weeks.

The sun rode high in the sky, bathing the small town of Whispsong in golden light. Within the Land of Grass, the afternoons always bordered on too hot. Looking up, Ilyas squinted his Silver eyes as he searched for any sign of rain. He rolled his shoulders, then tucked his wings tightly against his back because not a single cloud met his questing gaze. Rain would have meant there'd be fewer people out and about. Ilyas didn't like crowds. Someone always took issue to his wings, which clearly marked him as a High Fae from the Land of Vine. So far, no one in Whispsong had made a loud fuss about it, but it was only a matter of time.

Unfortunately, he couldn't delay this trip any longer. He had some skins already turned into leather and some that could go to the tanner, but those could wait. The damn mouse could not.

The buildings of Whispsong were squat, more long and square than those back home in Vine. There, everything was built high in the giant jungle trees that blocked out the sun. Here, sun was *all* there was. Endless savannahs of swaying grass extended in every direction, and all the houses were whitewashed and blinding. It was the same with clothing, and though Ilyas wore a cream tunic and a pair of thin, light blue pants that hung to mid shin, the illusion of fitting in wouldn't survive a second glance. Under the baggy pants—a year or two behind in style—and the shirt—more patches than whole cloth—he had a warrior's body. Vine Fae were built for combat, and while the locals of Grass could shapeshift into ferocious fighters, Ilyas still towered over them, even without his wings. If he was lucky, though, he would be in and out before anyone noticed that Ilyas didn't belong.

As he moved into town, the villagers were hard at work weaving, sewing, or dying cloth. Lesser faeries—an odd assortment of tiny winged skitterlings, knee-high crystalline druzies, and willowy tree-like mosskin—were scattered among the High Fae, silently laboring at their side. The lesser fae were normally not a bother, but as of lately the skitterlings in the area had been more of a pest then normal. Ilyas would have blamed them for his missing food, but his protective wards had kept them out of the cave. One skitterling in particular buzzed in front of his face, speaking in its high-pitched foreign tongue. Ilyas understood none of it. He swatted the creature away.

The first stall he stopped was willing to buy his skins. When he received back half the expected profit, he gave the man a confused look. "Why so low?"

"Haven't ya heard? War's a'comin' again. High King Ashan of Vine has taken Sunreach and plans on replacing Queen Maribell's hold on the Land with a puppet King of his own," the stout man explained, with a shake of his head.

Ilyas scowled. The death of the Mad Queen Maevian had left the Plane of Zenith, and him in particular, with problems aplenty. Did her son really have to pick up her mantle? Idiot.

Not just her son. Your son, my Silver Shade, a sneering voice whispered out of his past, but Ilyas pushed it away. Just because he had sired the boy, it didn't make him responsible for Ashan's choices now that he was full grown.

Snapping out of it, Ilyas sighed, then nodded to the merchant. "That will do, then. Thank you." It all sounded like things best left to those who wanted to be involved. His cave was simple enough for him to enjoy some peace and quiet, and never be bothered again. Of course, these days his cave wasn't quite the haven it had been for the past year.

At the general store, Ilyas stopped at the counter and grunted, "Mouse traps?"

The clerk pointed to a nearby shelf. "Got a rodent problem?"

"Hope so," Ilyas answered, because there was one other likely reason his food stores kept dwindling faster than he ate them, and he didn't feel like bloodying his knives inside a thief. Ilyas was *trying* to do less killing these days.

The clerk leaned on his counter, smoking a cigar from Herb by the smell of it. "I do as well. Nuisances. You should get a cat. Say," he paused, "I've seen you around a few times now, stranger. I'm Gremal. What's your name? Live nearby? You shouldn't be out there alone. We've had a rash of Feral sightings the past few days." The man took a long puff of his cigar. Blowing out the smoke, he continued, "I'm hoping they stay away, but I'd suggest taking precautions. We have some Violet-strength ward-staves piled in the center of town. You may want to stay close by, just in case."

Ilyas tried to suppress a grimace at the inane chatter. "I can handle Ferals. It's other people I want nothing to do with."

"Fair enough. I thought I'd offer to send my lad around with an Evergreen vermin-catching spell, but it sounds like you aren't keen for company. Looking for anything else?"

Ilyas hesitated, his desire to stay out of current politics warring with his need to know if there was a threat coming his way. "Heard about King Ashan's conquest of Grass. Is he doing it the same way the Mad Queen did?"

Even asking hurt, but he had to know. If his long-estranged son was Bonding his soldiers and citizens against their will to use them in the meat-grinder of Vine expansionism, Ilyas would have to go back and kill him, too. He had spared the boy after killing his mother, but only because Ashan had been a child at the time. He had hoped, vainly it seemed, that Ashan wouldn't follow in his mother's footsteps.

"Haven't heard that in particular, but who knows with Vine. No offense, of course, but your people are..." the shopkeeper gestured vaguely in the air with a pudgy hand, "known to go to extremes."

Ilyas grunted. "Any sightings of Willow of Herb, with Vine on the warpath again?"

Gremal shrugged. "The Warden? None that I've heard. Come to think of it, I'd really expect to. Wonder what ever happened to that one?"

With no answer to give or inclination to theorize about his old enemy turned uneasy ally Ilyas finished his shopping, handed over the majority of the money he had just earned, and left. He had reached the edge of town when a rock bounced off the back of his head, causing him to swivel around, Silver eyes searching the street.

"Go back to where you came from, Vine scum," a man's voice called out, but he was either smart or cowardly enough to not show himself. Ilyas's hands contracted into fists in his pockets, but he did not summon his knives, or turn towards the source of that voice. He didn't even twitch his aching wings.

Instead, he knelt and picked up the pebble,

hefting it in his hand. Smooth, flat. It would be a good rock to skip across a lake. Or hit a mouse.

He slipped it into his pocket and walked out of Whispsong.

Once he was out of immediate sight of the town, Ilyas stretched his wings wide. He hated keeping them so tight against his back, but it was the only way he could be certain no one would recognize him. If they did, there would be trouble, and he had done so well for the past year. After working the soreness out of his wings, he let a bit of Essence call a breeze under them to help lift him off.

As he flew, Ilyas studied the landscape. Near the border of Vine and Grass, rocky and jagged mountains formed a barrier. He had always wondered why the savannah that was Grass led into mountains, which gave way to a thick and untamed jungle. Yet, that was the way the border between some Lands worked. He had long ago decided that such details were beyond him. Matters of war, matters of killing... Those he knew well.

He landed a short way away from his cave. It wasn't too high in the mountains, but the way was difficult enough to climb for someone who couldn't fly. Out of the corner of his eye, he noticed the faery ring that had appeared a few weeks ago was still there, blue crystals glittering in the sunlight on the valley floor. Damn lesser faeries. Couldn't the blasted creatures leave his corner of the wilderness alone? Maybe that was where all the excess skitterlings buzzing around the cave had come from.

Carefully, he walked along the jagged ledge that led to his home, testing each place he set his foot before putting his weight down. It wouldn't be the first time the ground fell from under his feet, too dry and brittle to hold his weight.

At the entrance, he stopped and listened. It was reflex by then, so Ilyas actually twitched when a noise broke the expected silence. It was faint, but something, or someone, was inside his cave. He considered the rock for a moment, before deciding that his hands would do just fine. With quiet, slow steps, he closed his eyes and walked into the darkness. He had deliberately left things out to trip up potential intruders. Yet he had memorized every inch of his domain, knowing full well where each obstacle lay. Including his stores of food.

As he crept closer, the sound became louder. Enough for him to make out that it wasn't a mouse. No, it was the worst kind of vermin: a thief. His jaw tightened. *Give them food, and then get rid of them if they are young... if not...You don't want any trouble, and a shallow grave is easy to dig...* he thought, stalking closer and closer to the unwary thief. How long had it been since he had realized his stores were going missing? This had to have been one person —the amount was too small to suggest otherwise. How had they stayed hidden this entire time?

As soon as he was in easy reach of the thief, he conjured a ball of light behind his head, giving him a brief look at his prey.

She was short enough that at first he mistook her for a child, but her tattered clothes hung off a woman's curves. Her hands—tanned, freckled, and smudged with dirt—were wrist-deep in a bag of *his* rice. Rice that went flying when he grabbed her wrist. She screamed and stumbled back, turning towards him as she did so.

That was when he caught sight of her face. It was heart-shaped, and framed by coarse, shoulder-length blue hair. She might have been pretty, had her face not been grimy and twisted into an expression of terror.

His Silver eyes were full of anger as they met her fearful, Golden ones. It was like something had grabbed a hold of his whole being. An overwhelmingly pleasant feeling, like sitting next to a fire on a long, cold night, trickled through his veins. Forming in his limbs, that heat coursed through his body until settling over his heart, in the veritable roar of sensation of a SoulBond forming between a High Fae and the Ruler they were meant to serve.

The little mouse tried to yank away, and in his shock, his hand went slack. For a brief moment, his mind conjured the Mad Queen's face over this girl's. Instead of blue hair framing Golden eyes, he saw the long dark locks and Obsidian eyes. He could hear the roar of the waterfalls from the day Maevian Oriset had forced Ilyas to Bond with her at the center of the Land of Vine. He could smell the blood from when his fingers had wrapped around Maevian's throat, severing that Bond and freeing him.

Then he blinked, and all he could see were the

frightened eyes of the little mouse—and Queen—his soul had just been Bonded to without his permission.

"Not again," he growled, as he reached out to grab her with the speed only a Vine warrior could achieve. "Never again."

The Story Continues in
A Bond of Thread
Coming June 21st, 2021
Pre-Order Here:
https://books2read.com/u/3GAqDQ

AUTHOR'S NOTE

Thank you for reading *A Binding Day Truce*. We hope you enjoyed the short, and the preview for *A Bond Of Thread*. Reviews help indie authors more than you could imagine, so if you enjoyed your foray into *The Mountain Fell*, please let us know.

If you'd like to be notified of new releases, get exclusive sneak peeks, and lots more, you can do so on any of the platforms below:

Plot Mom Discord: https://discord.gg/JzJJjQ6EZT
Plot Mom Youtube: https://www.youtube.com/plotmom
Facebook: https://www.facebook.com/authorallegra, https://www.facebook.com/JPBurnison
Twitter: https://twitter.com/AuthorAllegra
Patreon: https://www.patreon.com/PlotMom
Website: https://www.aocollectivepublishing.com/

AUTHOR BIO

Allegra Pescatore & J.P. Burnison are a pair of role-players turned authors, who write Fantasy, Science-Fiction, and LitRPG as part of the group of authors known as Ao Collective Publishing, with a focus on diverse characters, unusual worldbuilding, and dynamic collaboration. Allegra is the author of *Where Shadows Lie* and *NACL: Eye of the Storm*. Together with E. Sands, the co-author of NACL, and others, they are launching a brand new series in 2021, of which *The Binding Day Truce* is a prequel. Find out more at https://www.aocollectivepublishing.com/

Books by Allegra Pescatore:

NACL: Eye of the Storm: https://storyoriginapp.com/universalbooklinks/627b9b66-1fc3-11eb-8ff0-fb808f8f9977

Where Shadows Lie: https://storyoriginapp.com/universalbooklinks/de7fbcee-89b7-11ea-a046-3750c858784e

Solace of Memory (free): https://storyoriginapp.com/giveaways/eb39f972-3cd6-11eb-ac32-4b123ad8d8eb